playtime's over

playtime's over

James Kinsley

propolis

First published in 2021
by Propolis Books

The Book Hive,
53 London Street,
Norwich, NR2 1HL

cover photo & design by Niki Medlik
www.studio-medlikova.com

A CIP record for this book
is available from the British Library

ISBN 9781916905108

Designed and typeset by benstudios.co.uk

Printed and bound by TJ Books Limited,
Padstow, Cornwall

For Dan

1

It was dark. And it was cold. And Will could feel every pinprick of that cold sensation through his clothes, the clothes that were dragging him downwards. He could see, as if looking at himself from a vantage point six feet above, his body slowly start to spiral. The struggle had gone out of his limbs, the bubbles had stopped escaping from his mouth, the light had gone from his eyes. He watched himself raise a hand and, even as his body sank further, begin to forlornly wave. Wave at the him who wasn't there, who wasn't really watching him from a vantage point six feet above, because there was only one Will. The one in the body, the one drowning. The one letting himself drown. The one drowning himself. And as the waters grew darker, and colder, and Will sank further and further, he smiled to himself. A simple smile. The contented, unexcited, accepting smile of the person who wants to die, and who knows that shortly, very shortly, extremely shortly, he will do so. Will was dying, because Will was killing himself, because Will wanted to die.

In many ways, Will wanting to die and Will making himself die – killing himself, we should call it killing himself – was a break from his normal pattern. If wanting things to be a certain way and having the agency to make them that way was a habit Will could have formed earlier, it would probably have resulted in Will not killing himself. As he sunk (still waving, he noticed) he reflected on whether this was something those who knew him would appreciate. Would they think, "Aha, that's a shame. If Will was as good at paying those bills, or forging those relationships, or exhibiting a moral compass, or affecting some kind of positive change in the thoughts and attitudes of others, or playing an active role in his community as he turned out to be at killing himself, then he probably wouldn't have killed himself. I wonder if he thought about that." And, to be fair, Will had thought about it. He was thinking about it now. But the truth was that those other things, those cumulative little acts of betterment had always seemed so hard and unachievable. Whereas this one big act, this grand and futile gesture, this end to all sorrows, was deceptively easy. The end of everything, for the sake of a large weight, a small boat and a few knots. The effort it takes to perpetrate one large and momentous act is vastly outweighed by that which it takes to achieve a thousand small ones, it seems.

Will had wondered if he would see fish. If they would nose around his sinking body, curiously prodding him. He had even wondered, he was embarrassed to admit to himself, if he would see a dolphin, or porpoise, as he had heard such things swam in the waters around here. But it was night-time and there was very little light to penetrate down into the water. And besides, this was the North Norfolk coast, not some tropical scuba-diving hotspot. He might, if he was still alive, see a crab when he hit the seabed, but that was the likeliest of a very unlikely set of possibilities. The most probable outcome he realised was that he would soon be dead and it wouldn't matter, and as much as he had daydreamed about the possibility of fish when putting this final expedition together, not seeing them was okay.

It was so very cold and, much like his vision, Will's thinking was starting to go fuzzy around the edges. He thought for a moment about his mother, but this set his mind in a direction he did not wish to pursue, so he very deliberately stopped thinking about her. Instead he thought about Isobel, and what her reaction to his death might be. He disappointedly concluded that it probably wouldn't be all he had hoped for, a realisation which may have weakened the resolve of a lesser man to carry on drowning. But Will felt himself an old hand at disappointment, and persevered. Wasn't it, after all, disappointment that had brought him out here? To kill himself.

It was at that moment that his body decided it was time for his mouth to open, his lungs to scream, his arms to flail, legs to kick, and his mind to burst.

2

Will's eyes opened, and then he sat up, leaned forward and coughed, and then he was sick. He leaned back. His breathing was laboured. This was not, in itself, something Will was unused to, but it did strike him as puzzling at this moment. Not so much that it was laboured, but that it was happening at all. One of the first assumptions he had made about killing himself was that at such time as he had successfully ended his life, he would no longer be alive. And yet this breathing seemed to belie that assumption. He allowed himself a desultory swear.

He looked around, up and down the ... pier. The pier, on which he now found himself sitting. It was daytime, it was not unduly cold, even if it was not remarkably warm, and he was alone. On the entire pier, he was alone. Not a soul. Not a man, woman, child nor beast. No fishermen, pensioners, or purveyors of ice cream. Not even a dog.

"Spooky, innit?"

Will spun around to face directly behind himself, the one place he had not looked. He wasn't, it turned out, alone after all. There was a man. A man in a brown jumper and a flat cap. The jumper was a V-necked sweater, and Will couldn't help but notice that it was slightly too tight for the man, although nothing would have compelled him to mention it. The flat cap Will liked. It too was brown, and tweed, offsetting the man's fine beard, giving him a look of solid dependability. He looked like the sort of man Will aspired to be, the sort of man that Will was most definitely not. The man was also wearing a pair of jeans, of a shade of blue that was defiantly removed from the fashion, yet not so far as to be unfashionable. Cut neither too tight nor too loose, they were the epitome of 'functional', and added themselves to the air of reliable usefulness cultivated by the cap and brown jumper, but almost destroyed by the absurdly bright and colourful trainers beneath. If pushed to observe anything else, Will's next stop would have probably been to realise that the man's fine brown beard was slowly being infiltrated by bright white hairs. But Will settled for a guilty conversational gambit instead. "What?"

"I said," replied the man, with the air of someone talking to a simpleton, "that it's spooky, isn't it."

6

"What is?"

"The pier."

"Is it?"

"On account of there being, save you and I, no bugger on it."

"Ah. Yes, well."

"Tea?"

"I beg your pardon?"

"You, chap, are proving an irritation." The man leaned over, a forced politeness not quite disguising his impatience. "Would *you*," he said, pointing at Will, so as to avoid any further uncertainty, "like a cup of tea?"

"I don't… I think… Yes?"

"Is that a question?"

"Is what a question?"

"'Yes'. Or, as you put it, 'yes?'."

"Yes. I mean, tea."

"Fucking extraordinary," the man muttered to himself, before pointing to a café at the entrance to the pier. "There is tea in there. I intend to procure some. If that sounds satisfactory, you could join me and we could continue this conversation in a warmer locale."

The man made a deliberate and decisive move towards the café. Will made some less certain and more confusing moves to catch up with him.

There was a waiter in the café, who made Will and the man a cup of tea each.

"I'm Will." Will held out his hand, as he had seen more confident people do in similar circumstances. The man looked at him with an expression on his face that suggested amusement and took his hand lightly. He paused, as if enjoying the quaintness of the gesture, before firmly shaking it, and then letting it go.

"Viktor."

"Pleased to meet you, Viktor."

"You might not be."

"I'm sorry?"

"You might not be that either."

Will frowned and let the comment pass. This felt like the sort of conversation where it might pay to converse less and let the more confident participant do most of the heavy lifting. Instead, he opened a small sachet of sugar and poured the contents into his tea. He stirred, lifted, sipped and immediately bit back the instinctive satisfied exhalation associated with tea drinkers. It was something Will abhorred in himself, which like most things he abhorred in himself, he failed to notice or be bothered by in others. Viktor, three sugars, took a manly gulp of his tea, and did not let self-consciousness stifle his accompanying, "*Ahhhh.*"

"Have you ever thought," asked Viktor, "how good tea is? I mean, really thought about it?"

"Have I? No. Well, I mean, not really. Is it something you think about?"

Viktor looked at Will and nodded. "Think. About it."

Will looked down at the cup in his hands. The tea was warming a chill that he had realised was starting to pervade him. The cup gently steamed, and the sweet smell of the sugary drink was indeed pleasant. They were sat by a window, which had begun to steam up from the contrast between the heat of the café and the late afternoon cold outside. Will took another mouthful of tea and let himself think about the taste as the liquid warmed his mouth, swirled over his tongue and then slid down his throat. He noticed not only the taste, but also the sense of wellbeing that the familiarity brought him. Afternoons in cafes such as this, a mug of tea, a window to look out of. Tea. Milk. Sugar. Steam. Warmth.

Will thought about the lunchtimes spent with friends in cafés in town, bunking off school, spending their pocket money and avoiding their lessons. Teas made by roommates at university, to fuel an essay or ease a hangover. Teas made by Simon, on the endless, carefree afternoons of their early twenties, playing video games or watching cartoons. A never-ending, rushing cascade of tea, covering his life and sweeping all those moments up and carrying them downriver to the tea sea, that repository of memory that stretches to the horizon and…

Viktor leaned across the table and snapped his fingers twice in Will's face. In his other hand, he was brandishing a packet of cigarettes. Will started as he realised he was being offered one, indoors. As if it were the olden days.

"In here? Really?"

Viktor, with the ease of the magnificently gifted, gesticulated wordlessly, conveying that it was probably alright, he didn't think it would be a problem, in fact he was sure it wouldn't be, and that he, Viktor, was going to have one, and that Will should have one too, but if Will didn't, well, that was okay, and anyway, look, the man behind the counter obviously doesn't mind, and there is no-one else in here. It was a hand gesture that defied belief in its intelligibility and that, as much as anything, shocked Will into taking one. Viktor withdrew the carton in the instant that Will took hold of the extended cigarette, effectively drawing it from around the cigarette with no need for Will to move, and returned the packet to his pocket from where he retrieved a lighter and ignited. The flame flickered gently, waiting for Will to insert his cigarette into it and inhale.

"I mean, if you're sure…"

"Will. I've never been more sure."

Will leaned in and lit his cigarette, closing his eyes as he inhaled, embracing the smoke within himself, the taste and *ohhhhhh* the hit. He opened his eyes wide. Much as he had with the tea, he found himself thinking of every morning, afternoon, evening and night-time cigarette he had ever smoked. The drunk cigarette, the hungover cigarette, the toilet cigarette, the work break cigarette, the behind-the-school cigarette, the stolen cigarette, the tea-and-cigarette cigarette, the angry cigarette, the loving cigarette, the hollow, sick-making cigarette, the depressed cigarette, the Oh my God are you still here and why are you looking at me like that I just want a fucking cigarette cigarette. The first cigarette he shared with his father. The last cigarette he shared with his father. The cigarette he'd smoked in that way to look like Gary Oldman in that film. The cigarette he'd smoked the night that Gavin had died. His very first, stolen, cigarette. His very last, borrowed, cigarette.

"I shouldn't really, I'm supposed to have given up."

Viktor stared at Will in disbelief. "Is that a joke?"

Will squinted quizzically at Viktor.

Viktor looked at him and gestured with his hands. "What do you think I'm doing here, Will? This," he waved again. "What did you think all this was?"

"A café?"

"Fuck me, Will, you are spectacularly dense. Now smoke the cigarette. And *remember* the cigarette."

Will smoked it. And remembered it.

3

On a beach, Will noted. We're now standing on a beach. He looked over at Viktor, who had his back to him. Legs wide apart, hands on his hips, Viktor was gazing out to sea, and Will suspected that the stolid, manly pose was both deliberate and rather over-egged.

The day was somewhat overcast with the sun trying to break through, and a thin lip of white water at the point the sea met the sand, as the waves struggled to justify their name. Off in the distance Will could see boats, old-fashioned sailing vessels, he realised. There was what looked like a tall tower, also in the distance. The beach was largely deserted, although there were four people stood by an assortment of baskets a short way from Will and Viktor.

"Where…?"

Viktor turned to face Will and held a finger to his lips. He made a gesture with his hand, as if to say, 'Take in the silence, smell the air, breathe deep and find your own definition of where you are.' Will, again mesmerised by the communicative capability of a waved hand, nodded. He closed his eyes and took a long, deep breath, and as he did so, the smell of saltwater fired his synapses with sensation and memory, triggering images of holidays and day trips and evening drives and dunes and picnics and bonfires and kites and sandcastles and frisbees and ice creams and donuts. His ears were suddenly as if flung open to the sound of the breakers and gulls, and the breeze that was raising the hairs on his arm, sending up a frisson of thrill which made his chest shudder with pleasure. Will opened his eyes and drank in the colours, the movement of the clouds, the ebb and flow of the sea, the huge, huge sky and the far-off horizon.

"That's where." Viktor was grinning at him, and Will grinned back as his whole body, awash with sensation, remembered what it was like to truly be aware of his surroundings. Viktor pointed at the tower in the distance and, more prosaically, said "Yarmouth. Late 1820's."

"What?"

Viktor, now turned fully and beside Will, leaned in and tapped him on his forehead. "All in here, isn't it. Remember?"

"I say, excuse me."

A new voice, the first Will had heard since the pier. He looked round, the surprise evident on his face. A young man with curly hair and dressed in an outfit that Will, in his ignorance, could only have described as 'old-fashioned' was sat on a folding stool. The young man pointed at the group of people by the baskets which, Will noted, required the man to essentially point through him. He held a sketchbook in his hand.

"Ah, sorry, in the way, I see. Sorry."

Viktor, holding Will's arm, steered them away and behind the man, who returned to his sketchbook. Viktor was grinning, inanely, Will thought. Will shot him a quizzical look, as if to say 'Am I missing something?' Viktor raised his eyebrows and indicated with a flick of his head the people by the baskets. "Look."

"I am…"

"No, *Look*."

Will turned back to the group on the shore. To the left of the group, an assorted pile of baskets and coats and rope. Kneeling on the ground with her back to Will and Viktor, a figure, presumably female, in a rose-coloured skirt appeared to be adjusting the dress of a woman with a yellow shawl who stood facing them. The standing woman also had a large bonnet, a blue ribbon just visible over the brim. In front of her stood a man, shorter than the woman, in trousers, a white shirt and a hat that were all too big for him. His face was shadowed by the brim, but his relative height and outsized clothing made Will consider the possibility that he was a child. The group as a whole appeared to be waiting as the fourth figure, strangely familiar to Will, emptied fish from one basket into another. This person, male, weather-beaten and old, was dressed in a vivid orange jumper and topped off with a loose, ill-shaped blue and white hat, traces of red visible in the design. The hat. The hat...

"Ohhh."

Viktor's grin widened. "Exactly."

"Yarmouth, late 1820s. *Yarmouth Sands*, in fact. 1829."

"There, or thereabouts."

"So that man...," whispered Will, pointing at the fellow with the sketchpad.

"Joseph Stannard." Viktor, his hand once more on Will's arm, led him away down the beach. "Tell me about him."

"Born in 1796..."

"Seven."

"Born in 1797, died in ... Ah. Not long after painting this, I think."

"Tuberculosis. Probably let's gloss over that."

"Prominent member of the Norwich School, paintings include *Yarmouth Sands* and the magnificent *Thorpe Water Frolic*, a painting which I…"

"… Spent many a happy hour gazing at in the Castle gallery."

"Why didn't you take me there?"

"To the frolic? Too many people. Besides, the beach, the open air, isn't this… heavenly?"

"Heavenly? You mean…?" Will looked round sharply, as if expecting the appearance of angels at any moment.

"Figure of speech. You're still drowning. Not dead yet!" Viktor punched Will playfully on the arm, causing him to wince.

"So why?"

"Why what?"

"Don't be dense. The boat, the jump, the …" Viktor waved his hands in front of his face, in some ghastly pantomime of '*drowning man*'.

"Don't you know?"

"Well, yes, I'm just not sure if you know. Really."

Will didn't reply for a moment. He looked back at Stannard, and then out to sea. "I know," he said finally.

"Okay, so if you know why you're doing it, maybe I just want to know if you know, really know, what *it* is that you're doing."

"Killing myself?"

"But what it is. What it means. It's an end, Will. An end to all this. Every last thing on Earth that gave you pleasure, even if you spent so much time thinking about what gave you pain. Maybe I just want to remind you of the things you're not thinking about."

"That sounds ghastly."

"Fuck off. Want to see the finished painting?"

Will looked down the beach. He took another deep breath of sea air and watched as the sun broke through the cloud cover, visible shafts of light hitting the beach. He listened to the gulls flying overhead, their distinctive bark on the breeze. Crouching down, he took a handful of sand, and let it trail through his fingers. "I don't like sand," he whispered to himself, a smile on his lips.

Viktor clapped him on the shoulder, "I know, it's coarse and it gets everywhere. C'mon, champ."

4

The gallery was silent. This particular gallery, in the heart of a museum in the heart of a city, a museum encompassing both local and natural history, as well as a busy cafeteria, was often quiet. Dressing up as a Roman or looking at the marks in the wall made by prisoners, or pressing the buttons to activate the birdcalls in the zoological dioramas were the popular draws for the parties of schoolchildren that made up most of the weekday trade. A collection of old paintings by a group of artists that many locals didn't even know were part of their heritage was not the centre-point of the collection. And if Will was honest, much as he bemoaned the city's indifference to that part of its history, the solitude afforded him in those cool rooms did, in many ways, make up for it. But this wasn't just quiet, it was actual silence. Will was acutely aware that no person other than Viktor was even remotely audible, not even distantly.

He and Viktor stood by Stannard's painting of *Yarmouth Sands*, even after all these years the vivid blue of the old man's hat a startling splash of colour amidst the soft shades of the beach scene. He marvelled, as he often did, at the enormous sky, and the one small concentrated area of detail that the small party with the baskets constituted. It was, he had always thought, a beautiful scene. Maybe not one that grabbed you, or shouted for attention, being largely an empty beach and a totally empty sky. But one that quietly drew you in, that modestly bequeathed its vision onto those who took the time to pause before it. The smallness of the people against the vast emptiness of the setting being the scene's elegantly made point.

They stood there for a few minutes, before Will wandered over to another painting. "You know, this was the one that first, suddenly, brought home the significance of this collection to me."

Viktor took a pair of spectacles out of his pocket and put them on, leaning in to read the label. "*Station Road, Brundall*. John Joseph Cotman. 1850."

A pastoral scene, a road heading downhill away from the viewer, towards a broad. A house just visible behind some trees, in the mid ground. On the road, central to the painting, in the foreground, a stout fellow carrying a bundle of sticks walks next to a small boy. The boy is leaning out and pointing at something, whilst the man stoically plods along with his burden.

"When I started going to school in the city, I used to walk down that road every day to catch my train. And yet here we are a hundred and twenty years earlier, and the same scene, different in so many ways, but definitely recognisable, was the subject of a painting by an artist who formed part of a movement which was both defiantly local and yet of national significance. This ... backwater that I always assumed I lived in, had more to offer than I'd ever imagined, and seeing this painting here, of my home... Well, it moved me."

Viktor eyed him sideways and nodded. "So I see."

"It drove me to find out more. John Joseph Cotman. John Sell Cotman. Stannard. John Crome. I learned about them, read about them, came back here time and again to consume these paintings. I..." Will stopped, put a finger to his lips. Then he spun around and walked off, into the central room of the gallery. Viktor coughed once and followed.

"So this is the ploy. Make me think about art, relive memories of the beach, make me think about all the things I love and convince me to return above. To kick out and swim for shore."

Viktor checked his watch. "I don't know that at

21

this point we're really talking about options, so much as some final clarity, but okay. Sure. If you like."

They moved to stand in front of Stannard's huge *Thorpe Water Frolic, Afternoon*. The Yare choked with boats, with sails. If you stood looking at it for any length of time, Will felt, you would start to hear the shouting and splashing. Twenty thousand people, of a town whose population was only fifty thousand, would congregate by and on the river, and Stannard's painting conveyed some of that thronging, that intimate and infectious chaos. It never failed to make Will stop in his tracks when he walked into the room. He stood now, gazing at the detail, whilst Viktor looked down, and then around, and then stepped back to sit on a bench. Will, as he always did, picked out Stannard himself in the picture, then turned round to look at Viktor. Did he look slightly… fatter? Was the jumper a little tighter? Will was certain that the hair underneath the natty brown cap was visibly longer than when they had stood on the pier. Viktor looked up at him. "Hmmm?"

"Nothing." Will went to sit beside him, before redirecting his gaze back to the painting.

"So, what happened?"

"I'm not sure I'm inclined to talk about it."

"That seems both an absurd remark, and an ill-timed one, given the circumstances."

"But if you know?"

"Pretend I don't. I don't know…." Here, Viktor scratched at his beard. There was definitely more white in it now. "I think it's what we're about, in this moment. Be a shame to ignore the…" He waved his hand, indicating that this was a unique opportunity to take stock of all one's knowledge, review it and finally lay it all out in a grand, unified design.

"Would you stop doing that?"

"What?"

Will moved his hand in a vague, indeterminate fashion, conveying little if not nothing to Viktor. "That."

Viktor merely raised his eyebrows.

"Fine. You want to know why I jumped out of a boat and am drowning in the North Sea rather than sitting in a museum talking to some kind of solipsistic avatar of myself …" He wavered.

Viktor's eyes narrowed. "Go on."

"I think…" Will paused as his mind scrambled for some kind of explanation that would make sense. "I think that if you want me to see what the world has to offer, the positive things I'm electing to give up, then starting with really old things that I look at in order to escape from the world seems an odd place to start."

"Maybe I'm saving my most convincing arguments for a grand finale."

"Whilst I'm drowning? Nice."

"Come on, I could do with a walk."

The two men got up and left the gallery. There was no-one in the Central Rotunda, indeed no sign of anyone in the museum at all. Will, ever a creature of habit, walked into the gift shop and picked up a postcard of *Yarmouth Sands* and looked around guiltily as the realisation of having no form of payment dropped into his consciousness. Viktor tapped him on the forehead and shrugged. Will picked up a pencil with a knight on the end, pocketed the two items and together they walked out through the front door.

The castle sat on a tall, man-made mound that stood watch over the city. Will and Viktor walked around the top, pausing every now and then as Will saw some local feature that caught his eye. There was nobody up there with them, and the suggestion of people they saw in the city all moved with a vague uncertainty that cast doubt on them being anything other than background detail Will's mind was inserting for him. They stopped on the west side, looking out over the market and on to the Art Deco City Hall.

"This city voted to stay in the EU," said Will, after a while. "An island of Remain adrift on a sea of Leave."

Viktor nodded, and lit a cigarette.

"And that's why you wanted to kill yourself?"

"Of course not. I'm just saying."

"We were talking about why you wanted to die."

"Yes, well. I won't lie, there was something about all that that made the world seem like an awful and shitty place. Rampant nationalism, racial intolerance, toxic masculinity everywhere. Who could bear to live in a world where everyone defined themselves by who they hated?"

Viktor inhaled deeply and blew out a smoke ring that disintegrated almost instantly in the light breeze. "I imagine that would be utterly intolerable."

Will narrowed his eyes and looked at Viktor. "If you're just going to make fun…"

"No no, not at all, I'm just saying. Awful. Awful awfulness wherever you look. Must be a terrible thing to bear. Yet you managed it for forty odd years. Something must have changed. And are we really sure that this isn't more about you?"

"Maybe I woke up. Or maybe I gave up. I don't know." Will pulled out the postcard of *Yarmouth Sands* and his knight pencil, and scribbled something down. Then taking the postcard by one corner, closing his eyes and taking a deep breath, he asked "So if all this is in my head, then the rules of physics are overcomeable by my thoughts?"

"Overcomeable? Really?"

"Shut up. By my thoughts."

"Sure."

Will extended his arm suddenly, let go of the postcard and it flew, up and far and fast and impossibly, over the city and out of sight. He opened his eyes again and smiled. "Where next?"

Viktor looked at Will and made a gesture with one hand, causing Will to flip out of sight. He then pulled the postcard from his pocket and read the inscription. "Dear Nicky. I'm sorry. For all of it. Will."

Viktor looked up, as if trying to spot where Will had gone.

5

For a moment, Will thought they were on another, more pebbly beach, but the mist made it difficult to discern more than a few feet from where he and, now, Viktor stood.

"What kept you?"

Viktor smirked, and lit a cigarette.

"You smoke an awful lot of those."

"Perk of the job." Viktor tapped his chest. "No lungs." Viktor's smirk turned into a full-on grin and he exhaled a plume of smoke.

"So where are we then? Is this supposed to make me nostalgic for inhospitable, gravelly nothingness?"

As if prompted by Will's remark, the mist cleared a bit, revealing more inhospitable, gravelly nothingness, only now Will could see bits of barbed wire, as well as the steep slope they stood precariously near the top of. Viktor raised his eyebrows, in a *Get it now?* type of way. Will shrugged a non-committal shrug. Viktor pointed down the slope to where a small group of people became visible through the gloom.

"Another painting?"

Viktor shook his head and pointed at them again.

There were three of them, two men and a woman. One man was crouched at the feet of the other, tying his shoe, perhaps, or fiddling with something the taller man was stood on. The man on the floor was wearing a blue blazer, Will could see, and the taller man was dressed in reds and browns, behatted and sporting a ridiculously long scarf.

"Oh c'mon… Really?"

Viktor raised his eyebrows again.

"From nineteenth century Yarmouth to Skaro? So what's my lesson here?"

"No lesson. Well, not for you. Maybe one for me."

"Go on."

"You spoke of the evil in the world," Viktor smirked again. "This seemed a fitting locale. Talk to me."

Viktor sat down on the ground, his feet over the edge of the sharp drop. Will thought about it for a moment, then joined him. They watched the trio below finish with whatever it was they were dealing with, before tramping off into the fog.

"It's hard."

"What is? Talking about it?"

"Talking about it without sounding ridiculous, maybe. I mean more the living with it. The seeing it every day on the news, on the internet. This never-ending tsunami of bile and hatred and misogyny and racism. It just… never ends."

"Except, doesn't it?"

"How do you mean?"

"Does it go on at home? In your home, I mean. Or where you work? Amongst your friends? Are your friends like that?"

"No, my friends are decent people, it's not… okay, it's not everywhere."

"But you see it every time you look online, or read the news, or what have you."

"Exactly."

"Have you ever considered not doing that?"

"Not looking, you mean? Of course! Who doesn't? But you can't live like that, can you? Not taking anything in, not participating, shutting yourself off."

"Ah, the bubble."

"Yes, the bubble. The social bubble where you only interact with nice people and just ignore the rest. Just let the pricks get on with being pricks. But some people have to be out there, and if everyone else stays home, it's just them versus the pricks. Take this, for example." Will gestured at the scene around them. "When they first cast a woman in the role, the whole internet exploded with fury. Even the idea of a woman playing a part that had always been played by a man drove some people actually insane, despite there being no narrative reason why it couldn't be a woman, no reason at all. But these people! Calling themselves fans but without an ounce of love for the spirit of storytelling, who want their thing to be theirs and only theirs. These wretched gatekeepers screaming into the void, cursing and swearing at strangers, petitioning to ruin other people's fun, other people's careers and livelihoods. The rape threats, the death threats, the sheer fucking nastiness of people who hate anyone who's not like them. It's crushing."

Viktor leaned back, and eyed Will in a way that suggested he was seeing something he'd not seen before. "It troubles you that much?"

"Of course it troubles me! It's horrific. It makes me despair. And you suggest that I just turn it off and walk away? Pay no attention, let these people just get on with throwing this shit around?"

"Can you stop them?"

"Of course not! But if I'm participating, I'm at least making a different noise."

Viktor nodded, and leaned forward again, looking down the cliff.

"And it's not just that, it's everything, everywhere. Women being in things, wanting to do things, to say things, shouted down everywhere. And people of colour and the LGBTQ community, anything that's not a red-faced hetero white man shouting is just another thing for a red-faced hetero white man to shout at. And when you call it out, you're laughed at, get called a social justice warrior, or a snowflake, because giving a shit about your fellow man is something to be ashamed of. Apparently."

They sat for a minute, perhaps two, looking out into the mist. Or fog? Will wasn't sure which. Something to do with if you're on land or sea, maybe?

"Toxic masculinity in a nutshell."

"The whole 'What do you mean, I have to be nice to someone who's not me!' Pathetic." Will reached out and took the cigarette offered.

"So you think the best thing to do is shout back, be a positive voice."

"It must be. At the very least I can be part of the opposing noise. The positivity I want to see in the world."

"Well it's an honourable goal."

"You don't sound convinced."

"I'm just wondering, that being the case, why we're here."

Will's mouth opened to respond…

6

"That's…"

"Unfair?"

"Well, yes." Will found himself speaking up to make himself heard over the rumbling around them.

"Tough."

Viktor looked slimmer to Will now, the white almost non-existent in his beard, the lines around his eyes less pronounced. Even the frame under the brown jumper looked, if not leaner, more defined. Will frowned, and then his shoulders slumped. "It just got so hard, all the time, trying to be that voice."

"Oh, come on, no-one asked you to make the world a better place all by yourself."

"I know, but I can't take responsibility for anyone else's actions, so there's only my own left. It felt as if I could see what needed doing, but all I could contribute was my tiny part of it. How does anyone

look at the disparity between those things and not…
end up here? Where are we exactly?" Will looked up
and took in their surroundings. The Underground.
More specifically, according to the map above the
window, the District & Circle line. Viktor was dressed
as before, but now with a scarf, and seemed to be
associated with the large placard leaning on the seat
next to him. Whatever was written on it was facing
into the seat. Will was rather startled to find propped
next to his own seat a similar placard, which he now
instinctively thought of as 'his'.

"Erm…?"

"Soon enough, young fellow, soon enough."

It struck Will as unusual that they were heading
somewhere rather than just appearing where they
needed to be. He considered asking Viktor but found
himself slumping back down. He had got himself
stirred up, and the emotional wave, having passed,
left him weary. He suddenly felt thirsty in the hot
carriage and was less surprised than he would have
been earlier when, on having that thought, Viktor
passed him a bottle of water.

He took a mouthful, then another, and then
passed the bottle back. After a moment, the train
slowed, and pulled into a station. Will looked up
and saw that they were at Temple. The doors opened
and, after the usual interval, closed again. The train

33

was empty, so no-one got off. And as the station was empty, nobody got on either.

"It's funny," said Will, after a moment.

"Hmm?"

"I always slightly hated London, when I visited."

Viktor raised an eyebrow.

"I mean, don't get me wrong, I only came when I wanted to, and for things I wanted to see. And the things are great…"

"Oh yes," Viktor chimed in, "The things in London, those London things…" He raised a hand to his mouth and gave an exaggerated chef's kiss.

"Hilarious. No, I mean, to partake of all London has to offer, museums, galleries and the like, obviously wonderful, but the people… The crowds, the stench, the noise… I couldn't… you can imagine."

Viktor gazed at Will, their eyes locking, and nodded slowly.

"And yet, I never had that on the tube, despite the often-crushing presence of others. I think it's the order, the funnelling of that chaos into specific channels, designated routes, clearly identified stops. You get on here," Will pointed at the map, "and get off here," he pointed again, "and it's fixed. After here, it's here, and here, and here…" Each 'here' punctuated by his finger stabbed at the map. "It's comforting. Plus, we had that game when I was a kid."

Viktor leaned back, stretching, as the train pulled into Embankment. Train stopped, doors opened. Doors closed, train started. No people.

"Is made me take a bus once."

Viktor's face screwed up, and he turned to look at Will, with the appearance of someone who had smelt something both disgusting and confusing. "Say what?"

"Is. Isy. Isobel."

"Of course." Viktor's hand rotated in a fashion intended to convey that Will should, please, continue.

"I totally freaked out. Up there the roads all look the same, and the bus stops don't correlate to anything. It's just the name of a street…"

"Then it does correlate…"

"You know what I mean."

"Insufficient labelling?"

"Exactly. It's not a Location, it's just where you are."

Viktor's face, again, unconvinced.

Will slumped back again; his voice suddenly small. "I never know where I am on a bus. Unless I already know where I am. The bus offers no additional information to what I already know. But the tube, that map, that elegant design. To know that, is to have it all at your fingers."

"Can't get lost on the tube."

Will nodded and, realising that what he felt now more than anything was utterly lost, started to cry. The train pulled into Westminster. Viktor stood and took hold of his placard. Will, softly weeping, did the same. There seemed little alternative.

7

They ascended, emerging into a throng of people. Not *actual* people, Will reminded himself, as his breathing started to quicken. He glanced over at Viktor, who was definitely slimmer, younger. There was no white in the beard now. Again Will pondered the significance, until he was carried along down the pavement by a crowd that was crossing the road into Parliament Square. He then allowed himself a small moment of pride as he looked at all the wonderful individual people his subconscious had created. He had thought that the sparsely populated nature of his dying mind might reflect some dearth of imagination on his part, however it seemed that he was now capable of summoning vast hordes. But his pride soon withered, as it often did, the thought being swiftly pursued by the avenging beast of self-doubt, telling him that to feel pride in such a notion was, surely, ridiculous. So instead he flattened himself against the wall, allowing the crowd to drift past. Viktor, holding his placard aloft in one hand, the other displaying a thumb held high in an encouraging way, grinned wildly as he allowed himself to be swept along.

There were placards everywhere, but Will's imagination was clearly too engaged with creating a crowd to be concerned with writing slogans, because although the placards were definitely not blank, they never stayed still long enough for him to read them.

He looked again for Viktor and was startled to see him a lot closer than he expected; swept away as he had been, he nevertheless conspired to remain both close and highly visible.

"What's happening?" Will shouted, over the unintelligible hubbub of his chaotic mind.

"Protest, innit."

"Against what?"

Viktor was suddenly beside him, by a sleight-of-foot too mysterious for Will to grasp.

"That's the trouble, isn't it," Viktor suddenly seemed downcast. "It's always against something. Even when we protest for something, we talk about it in terms of what we're opposed to."

"I feel like you're filling in my arguments now. Aren't I the one supposed to be telling you this stuff?"

Viktor lit a cigarette and sat on a convenient

bollard. The hand that held the cigarette waved in front of his face for a moment, in a manner calculated to remind Will that he and Viktor were one and the same, and that to argue about who was having what thought was a needless exercise.

"It's easier," Viktor continued, "to be against something than it is to offer a sound, reasoned, workable alternative. That is why we protest *against*, rather than *for*. It's so often up to the other party to do all the heavy-lifting."

Will nodded.

"I'm afraid we're all culpable but It infuriates us when others do it," continued Viktor. "Take Britain's decision to leave the EU. Nothing more galling on earth than watching those utter bastards, who had spent twenty years campaigning for it, turning around after the referendum and washing their hands of any obligation to solve all the problems raised." He suddenly stood up and cupped his hands around his cigarette. "YOUR PEOPLE HAVE VOTED, PRIME MINISTER, WE ARGUED FOR IT! NOW MAKE THAT IMPOSSIBLE THING WORK PROPERLY!"

Will was gratified to see the nearest people, now forming the back line of a specific and largely stationary crowd, turn and look at the shouting man in the brown sweater. Extra points, he thought, for generating realistic crowd dynamics.

"But," said Viktor, taking his seat again and crossing his legs, creating a precarious balancing act for himself, "we all do it. A problem is something we identify, but usually expect someone else to have the responsibility of solving."

"I don't know that that's true," Will replied. "Some people are natural problem solvers."

Viktor squinted and looked up at the still standing Will. "But not us, eh, Will? Not the likes of you and I. Unless you call this a problem solved."

Will looked down at his feet. He knew what Viktor meant by 'this' and once again the reality of his failure threatened to swallow him whole. Did his trainers look… damp?

Viktor jumped back to his feet, albeit accompanied by a small stretch and old-man jig of back pain. "Bollards," he mouthed. Then, slapping Will on the shoulder, added "Come on you wee daftie, enough of that, you can't spend your last dying moments worrying about whether or not you should have killed yourself, I have a world of misery and wonder to show you yet."

Viktor upturned his placard and forced it into a nearby bin, before grabbing Will's and doing the same to that. He then pointed to a soulless multinational coffee chain and pulled Will towards it. "It's not tea on the pier, but it'll do."

8

They sat by the window, on a stool too high for comfort, at a ledge too narrow to be called a table, and supped at a drink too fussy to be called coffee. Much as he had with the tea, Will took a moment to recall his love of coffee, the switch at eighteen to having it without milk or sugar, the delight when he found what he considered to be 'his' brand of instant, the ceremony of putting a pot on after a meal with friends.

Other than the bearded, tattooed gentleman who served them, the coffeeshop was empty. Will was momentarily surprised by this, given the crowd outside, but realised that this arrangement was undoubtedly deliberate, their roles having changed from participants to spectators. He looked out on the throng, milling and shouting and waving, despite having no identifiable cause. His imagination was starting to cut corners now that the mob was at one remove, beyond the window. He almost expected to see people bumping into each other in the manner of clockwork automatons wound up and set off, with no agency of their own.

He accepted, without thinking, the cigarette Viktor held out to him and lit it.

"So what now? What's my next lesson?"

"You're becoming trite," Viktor responded. "I'd rather you didn't."

Will looked at him a moment, and then returned his gaze outside. "I feel as if we're waiting for something."

"We're waiting," Viktor replied, "for the *against*."

Will turned back to the window, biting his lip to avoid suggesting that *The Against* sounded like a tv show he'd check out just for the title. Viktor seemed keenly focussed on the crowd, and Will didn't think he'd appreciate the aside.

"You're right." Viktor tapped the side of his head, as a way to remind Will of their shared inner monologue, or dialogue. Thinking about that made Will remember where he was. Where he really was. His coffee had started to taste salty. He took another long hard pull on his cigarette to mask the taste of seawater, trying to ignore the fact that one of his feet was definitely starting to feel wet. Here. Here and now.

"It's amazing", he offered instead, looking down at the preposterous drink in his hand, "how much time and resource you can devote into spreading the wings of your coffee demon upon the world when you don't pay any tax."

"Really?" Viktor snorted. "Honestly, coffee chains not paying their taxes is five-years-ago's talking point. If you've nothing more to break the silence with, then perhaps best leave it unbroken."

"Didn't go away for the right reasons though, did it." Will stared despondently into his coffee as he carried on. "I mean, we didn't give them a break because they started coughing up."

"That's the runaway nature of the modern news cycle for you."

"If it's not new, it's not news."

"Exactly," said Viktor. "And you know why?"

Will swirled his coffee and took another swig. The brininess had dissipated, to his relief. "Because in the social media age, I am the news. And if I'm on social media sharing a story everyone else was sharing last week, then no-one's reading it. Today's story has even less relevance now than when being tomorrow's fish and chip paper was its fate. If I want people to pay attention to *me*, then I have to tell them something they've not heard before. We chase retweets like news broadcasters chase ratings."

Viktor snorted again.

"Quite," said Will. "And the result? No follow-through. You share something one day, but don't give it a second thought the next. Nobody has the time to debate anything, or pursue it, because no one still wants to be discussing it when everyone else has already moved on. And power ends up with those who can wave their tiny hands the fastest. The jester becomes the king."

Viktor stuck his cigarette between his lips and, eyes still on the crowd, offered Will a tiny, silent round of applause. "You should write that one down."

Will noticed that the crowd suddenly looked more purposeful again, focussed on something he couldn't see, down Abingdon Street. It was hard to identify what made the sound of unintelligible voices seem more pointed, but nevertheless, he could feel something in the air that wasn't quite electricity, but wasn't quite not electricity either.

"It's anticipation," said Viktor, squaring his cap more firmly on his head, before throwing back the remains of his coffee. He spun on his seat to face Will directly. "And so. In this world of ever moving news and the need to be first with it. What are you? The rock in the centre of the stream, not budging as the waters break around it and speed on? Or the pebble, washed downstream with the rest of the detritus?"

"If you're asking, am I guilty of the need to feel like I'm offering something new, to want to be the first to share the link? Of course. I've no illusion that I'm better than anyone else. I'm as pathetically self-serving..."

"No, no, no!" snapped Viktor. "We're not here so you can flagellate yourself, we're here so you can understand."

"And I do…"

"Then just say it." Viktor's finger stabbed at the centre of Will's forehead, eliciting a sharp cry of surprise and annoyance that Viktor ignored. "Admitting your weaknesses is not the same as relishing the recounting of them. Be honest not boastful. Nobody should boast about what an arsehole they are."

"I'm not boasting…"

"You're telling me something about yourself because you like the way the words sound. You're boasting. Now, are you defiant or complicit in the face of the need for the new?"

"Complicit."

Viktor cocked an eyebrow, one Will noticed now as having one or two errant, wayward hairs. The look was clearly an invitation for him to continue, but Will was wary of a trap, and so just nodded. Viktor maintained the look for a beat, then nodded as well. He extinguished his cigarette and stood up. "Out there," he pointed, "I am about to show you something that will seem absurd to the point of silliness, though it may not strike you as silly at first. But it ties this whole bit up." At the words 'whole bit', he circled an arm wildly, encompassing all that had transpired since they had found themselves on the tube. His eyes widened, unnerving Will, whose own eyes narrowed questioningly in return. "And then," Viktor concluded, "we'll perhaps get some lunch."

9

Will stood on the pavement and trembled, his body alive to the stench of the crowd, the shouting that, now they were amongst it again, seemed overwhelming. And angry. He could feel himself retreating within his head, no longer inhabiting the whole of his body, but a passenger, looking out through its windows. That was always his mind's first line of defence in the face of large numbers of people. It was bad enough, he shuddered to himself, at parties. And this was no party.

Viktor grabbed his arm, and thrusting Will in front of him, pushed on into the crowd. Will could feel the tension now, the focus of this crowd on another body of people coming, both literally and ideologically, from the other direction. The Against. His eyes wide now, he grabbed Viktor's wrist, the wrist of the hand that was, in turn, grabbing his, and spun round to look at the other man. He pleaded, with his stare, to be released, to go back, but Viktor, more well-built now, stronger, taller even, ignored him and pushed again. Pushed on, pushed further. Deeper. Feet, legs, elbows, hands, Will and Viktor pushed past, through and against body parts. Some people, their attention briefly diverted from their focus, shoved back. Others cursed. But most barely registered them, parting briefly to let them through, before swarming back together after they passed, leaving no gaps in the wake of the two men. Will could feel the sweat crawling down his spine, sweat from the heat, and from the fear. It wasn't just the fear of the crowd, it was more tangible, more exterior than that. It was fear of what was ahead of them, the confrontation that Viktor was pushing him towards.

Banners waved, placards were proffered and, despite Will's belief that such a thing was impossible, the crowd got tighter and tighter, until suddenly… Air! Still hot and fetid, but enlivened in a way that air in the knot of a mob is not. They burst through the front line, ejected unceremoniously by the crowd into the no-mans-land of the street, and Will shrank with terror at the sight ahead. Another mob, mere feet away, heading towards them. Will couldn't say how he knew, but he knew; whatever the crowd that had ejected him had felt like, the one now approaching was worse. There was a wave of stink, of lager and piss and hatred, that rolled before the oncoming herd like a tide of violence, making Will gag. He could see shaved heads, St George crosses, jeans and white t-shirts and tattoos, the homemade, aggressive kind. There were placards again, but these ones Will could read. They bore mainly racially-charged slogans, with the odd declaration that ALL lives matter. There were fewer women in this crowd. And behind it… Will almost fell to his knees, but Viktor yanked his arm hard and restored his footing. Will tried to turn away, to plunge back into the crowd that moments before he had feared so much, but Viktor spun him back around and grabbed his jaw, forcing his gaze up and back to the hellish image before him.

Looming above the crowd were five terrible, haunting figures. As Will looked on them, his fear knotted into something more vicious, a manifest hatred clenching every muscle of his being.

Like gruesome horsemen of a modern apocalypse, he recognised, and despised, what he saw. War, the bitter, ranting sociopath, one finger on the button, the other hand busy on a phone, as he spat forth insults and crudities. There was Famine, his frog-mouthed barking a call for action to set the poor against the poor. There was Pestilence, spewing her lies and bile at anyone who would listen to her toxic agenda.

Death, looming above them all, his desiccated, corpse-like figure moving only to shower his people with newspapers to blind and deceive them. And then the fifth figure, shiny, pudding faced, basking in the reflected glory of the others and echoing, amplifying their lies. Together they whipped their angry mob on and as Will watched, he felt his blood boil and suddenly wished for nothing more than to do harm in retribution. He howled, a lone, desperate, ugly howl into the void, then the two lines of people met and there was only chaos.

As the crowds clashed, two waves from conflicting tides, placards and banners sprayed in every direction like errant surf. Will felt a fist connect with his jaw, and instinctively kicked back in response. Deafened by a sudden smothering of his senses, he lurched forward and thrust his head into the chest of a snarling brute of a man, sending them both crashing into the fray. Will flailed and, suddenly, the tight pack of bodies dissipated. What had been two large, semi-solid objects crashing against each other became something more random, fast flowing, as the fighting became personal, more intimate, and the mobs' unified impact dissolved into a myriad of one-on-one brawls. Will grabbed a shirt in front of him and spun it round until the man wearing it lost his footing and sprawled onto the floor, allowing Will to sharply thrust his foot into the small of his back, eliciting a satisfying yelp of pain. Another figure crashed into Will, shoulder to shoulder, and he nearly fell. He flailed in retaliation, not knowing or caring which side it had marched with. He caught it a blow on the back of its head even as, at the same moment, a fist landed on his jaw. Will whirled around, looking for Viktor, but he was nowhere to be seen. That couldn't be right, he thought, in a panic. Viktor only existed as a construct of Will's mind, surely he must be here, surely Will could *command* him to be here. He spun round again, back in the direction The Against had come from, but there was no sign of Viktor, just a London street hosting a running battle between two animated crowds of angry people. There must be more to it than this, Will thought. This is not just two lots of people failing to understand each other. The Against marching to the beat of the Horsemen's drum, *they are wrong.* They *must* be. Around and around Will spun, looking for Viktor. Looking for what he realised now was the voice of reason he needed to make sense of this.

The brawlers ignored him now as he started to weave amidst the individual conflicts, trying to find his friend, his gaze constantly arrested at the sight of a particularly vicious fight, a young woman brandishing her placard as a club, a man with his arms wrapped firmly around the neck of an adversary, forcing him to his knees in a style Will imagined was remembered from wrestling matches enjoyed on television. Will suddenly ducked to one side as the pudding faced man ran past him, giggling with glee over the chaos. As it overtook him, Will was horrified to find himself unconsciously stooping to pick up a brick, incongruously abandoned in the thoroughfare, and heaving it after the cackling deviant. It struck firmly in the middle of the man's back and felled him like a tree. He rolled, before turning to hiss a fiendish gasp, admonishing Will for being no better than the people he espoused to condemn. Will, aching inside to pick the brick up again and smash the man's face to a bloody pulp, ran on, swallowing back the vomit that tried to force its way up and out of his mouth, in horror at the fury within him.

"Not very subtle, is it?"

It was if the crowd was instantly muted. Will stuttered to a stop and looked at Viktor, sitting on a bench, leaning forward, elbows on knees, hands together. Viktor looked up at Will and raised an arm, taking the cigarette from his mouth and gesticulating at the street scene, absurd in its silence yet still vicious in activity. Further down the road, Famine, frog mouth stretched in a hideous rictus led a baying mob over the side of Lambeth Bridge and down to a watery grave.

"Not," Viktor repeated, "very subtle at all."

Will swallowed, heart racing, dropped his hands to his knees, braced himself as he stood and then threw up onto the road. He was aware of being ignored – invisible to – the combatants in the Battle of Abingdon Street. He was a spectator again, and as he vigorously expelled all that hatred onto the ground, he felt weak, and started to cry.

Viktor got to his feet, walked over to Will and put a hand under his upper arm, in much the same place as when he had first thrust Will into the mob, but this time the gesture was one of sympathy. Nevertheless, it was with firmness that he hoiked Will to his feet and escorted him from the field of play. Sound was restored to the scene as they moved further away, returning to its previous level before quieting again with distance, meaning it got no louder, just more believable, until it started naturally to subside and, eventually, was silent.

Viktor offered Will a cigarette, and the two walked in silence for a short way.

"So what am I supposed to take from that? That everyone's as bad as each other? That both sides are to blame for this constant war of ideals?"

"Fine people on both sides? Fuck, no. A racist piece of shit is still a racist piece of shit, no matter how hard you want to punch him."

"But?"

"But wanting to punch him comes with a price."

Will stopped, took a determined drag on his cigarette and exhaled dramatically. "I never realised how much anger there was inside me, until I saw... them. *The Against.*"

"Can I say 'Not very subtle' again?"

"It's your vision."

"It's *your* vision," Viktor insisted. "In so far as any of this is my doing, I am essentially your doing." The waving hand, again, encompassed the world, and all it contained. "Ain't nothing out here that didn't come from in here." And again the hand finished waving with a firm tap on Will's forehead.

"Look," said Viktor, "You know what I'm getting at. You don't need me to spell it out. Even though you do seem to need me to tell you that you don't need me to spell it out."

"Say again?"

Viktor pulled a face.

"Alright," said Will. "It's complicated, is that it? Is that the grand lesson? There is wrong and right, there are opinions that are awful, and sometimes those opinions are held by people who are flat-out awful. Beyond redemption..."

"Ah, well..."

"Alright, not beyond redemption, but in any

event, simplistic in their awfulness. Just bloody wrong people. But that", Will sighed, "doesn't mean that just because I'm not them, I'm not also awful too."

"Bingo." Viktor punctuated this single word with a declamatory finger point.

"So what's the conclusion? Turn the other cheek? Put the flower in the muzzle of the rifle?"

"Turning the other cheek is, I think, more about how we should defend ourselves. You sometimes need to defend others, and defend ideas, in a different way to how you defend yourself."

"So sometimes I have to be awful, or I can inadvertently be awful by trying to be good, but even when I do that, I need to know I'm being awful." Will felt sick again.

"Sometimes standing up to hate involves hate, but you still need to acknowledge it's hate. And when you pick hate up, you have to know when to put it down again. There's always a price to pay, and just because you're motivated by good, doesn't mean you get a free pass."

"Well, gee." Will looked around for a bin to put his cigarette end in. Even in his own mind, throwing it in the street seemed a bit off.

Viktor looked witheringly at Will's hand, before slowly reaching over and plucking the cigarette end from his fingers and making a magicianly gesture over the still smoking butt. It burst, for one solitary moment, into flame, and then disappeared.

"You promised me lunch."

"I promised you lunch."

10

Will felt dizzy. The whirling around, the snapping from one place to another, the nagging sensation of his trainers being soaked through that never seemed to be the case when he looked down, all this was leaving him confused and disorientated. He now found himself sitting on a low wall, running alongside a triangular piece of grass, looking over at a fish and chip shop. He was home again, and Viktor was walking towards him, two packets under his arm, doubtless containing the lunch that Will now found himself desperately in need of. Viktor sat himself down beside Will with a noticeable middle-aged grunt, the brown jumper stretched tighter over middle-aged spread, the beard grey where it hung from his middle-aged face. He dumped one of the packets unceremoniously in Will's lap, who opened it and savoured the smell of chips, salt and vinegar. Perched on top of the chips was a large, battered sausage; from which he took a large, satisfying bite.

"Oh, my word…"

"Good, huh?" Viktor opened his own packet, artfully tossed a nugget of scampi into the air and caught it in his mouth, as if he had been practising his whole life.

"Magnificent."

"Simple pleasures."

Will nodded, and forked himself a mouthful of chips. Viktor tossed up another scampi, and then, for a few minutes, there was silence between them, as they ate.

Will considered, without instruction, as he imagined he was required to do, the many fish and chip meals he'd consumed over his life. Those with friends, those with partners, those with family. The childhood ritual of fish and chips on a Friday night, his father collecting them on the way home from work, which would be followed by a small bag of sweets or a chocolate bar, and the unsurpassed joy of a later bedtime. Juggling crumbling bits of battered fish on a bench by the sea, hands greasy, wind blowing hair into faces. Isobel warming plates in the oven whilst he drove up the road to the chip shop owned by the smiling Chinese couple who never seemed to charge the same amount for the same thing twice. The taste of a perfectly cooked chip, with the perfect amount of salt and vinegar. The little rush of excitement that came from a spontaneous decision not to cook that night. If given a choice of takeaway, Will's could be relied on to plump for pizza, but there was no escaping the unique joy to be found within the wrappings of a greasy piece of paper, harbouring its own golden treasure.

Viktor was watching him, Will realised, as he slowly came back to the present from his reverie.

"Simple pleasures," he agreed.

11

Through the town and down into the Cathedral Close, Viktor led Will in silence. Will wondered at the sense of withdrawal in his previously verbose companion as they walked through the Ethelbert Gate. The Close was deserted, and Viktor led them straight to the West Door and into the nave, the Caen limestone creating a lighter, less foreboding atmosphere than the city's other, Catholic, Cathedral. Viktor removed his cap as they entered, the gesture surprising Will in its automatic display of reverence. Viktor had not, Will thought, struck him as an especially reverent character.

Will followed Viktor down the nave, until they found themselves by the copper font, fashioned, as Will had read somewhere, from bowls previously used for making chocolate, a reminder of one of the city's many now-lost industries. Viktor took a seat on the end of a row, leaving no room for Will unless he were to squeeze past him, which Will imagined was not being encouraged. Instead, Will took a seat on the other side of the aisle.

It was no surprise to Will that Viktor had led him here. The reckoning was overdue. Will's relationship with the church was mixed, and at times strained, but never lost. His parents had made it a regular part of childhood; always with encouragement rather than strict order. When his elder brothers eventually stopped attending, it seemed to Will that his parents' acceptance of this made it tacitly clear that he too had a choice, and therefore with no sense of there being anything to rebel against, Will had not rebelled. There had, of course, been questions, doubts, periods of absence, and an ultimate realisation that man's interpretation of the divine was just that – interpretation – and could never be anything more. Nevertheless, tradition and an underlying belief still existed for Will, and therefore his actions, specifically those most recent, had left him wondering if it was he who had let God down, or the other way round.

"Perhaps," Viktor ventured, in response to Will's train of thought, "it's nothing more than that you have both forgotten how to talk to one another."

"I'm not sure one's encouraged to talk of God forgetting how to do something."

There was no response from where Viktor sat, obscured from Will's vision by the great copper font between them.

Will's mind wandered to a time he had sat in this very Cathedral, listening to a performance of Arvo Part's *Passio*, a piece of music that at the time Will had struggled to connect with, but that years later, he had listened to in its entirety whilst sitting on the beach at Lindisfarne, his hands bundled firmly into his thick coat as a harsh wind had mercilessly frozen him. The way he had been able, on that day, to free his mind of all internal narrative and let the music wash over him, *through* him, was a memory that froze him in his seat. He would struggle to hum even a bar from it, but the emotion that haunting piece of music had inspired in him, in that place and time, was, he now realised, seared within him. Appreciation of the divine through unconscious, abstract thought, was that the key to revelation?

"I think if you're putting it into words, you're not *not* putting it into words." Viktor interrupted him, having slipped unnoticed into the seat beside him.

Will fixed him with a dour expression.

Viktor raised his eyebrows, in a manner that suggested surprise at Will's chastising glance. "All I'm saying is, you may just be trying too hard to capture the intangible." Viktor patted Will's knee. "I'll be outside. When you're ready."

Will sat alone, head in his hands, and tried not to think of anything. But did, of course.

Was self-destruction the ultimate sin? The rejection of what was so often presented as God's greatest gift – life itself? Yet if God had a plan for all of us, did that not imply that Will's suicide was part of it, rather than an aberration? Can God's plan even have an aberration? And if life is not determined, but rather there is freewill, and God's interaction in the world amounted to nothing more than the moving of men's souls, then was Will's suicide an indication that God had failed to give Will either the strength equal to his tasks or the tasks equal to his strength?

There was a painting in the nave that Will often gravitated to, and he shuffled down the seats now to put himself near to it. A depiction of Christ and a group of saints, on a featureless landscape against a black sky, the figures themselves reminiscent of centuries-old iconography. The dark sky and elaborate halos often, in Will's more irreverent moments, made him think the painting looked as if it was of biblical astronauts, in robes and fishbowl space helmets, hanging out on a desolate moon. He had at first felt guilty for the thought but had grown accustomed to it and now assumed that God, if He was any kind of being at all, would appreciate the joke. In any respect, as failings go, it was far from Will's worst.

He looked at the picture now and found that it gave him some comfort. The rudimentary rendering of an undeniably vague scene served to remind him that theology was, itself, no more than a rudimentary rendering of something infinitely more complex and unknowable. Will could hardly be expected to understand exactly how God would react to his taking his own life, other than being deeply saddened and hopefully anxious to restore peace to him. It was little more than Will's own interpretation of the Divine, but if God was doing anything in Will's soul, then maybe He was putting the thought there.

Will stood up, suddenly conscious of an ache throughout his body. He left the Cathedral by a side door, stepping into the cloisters.

Viktor was sat in an archway, looking out onto the green space before him.

"Answers?" he asked.

"Just more questions," Will replied.

"'Twas ever thus."

"I don't know the answers. But perhaps I don't need to. Or I'm not supposed to. We're taught from a young age that religion is an experience of answers, because those who espouse it don't want to appear foolish, and those whose job it is to draw in new followers want to have something to promise beyond doubt and confusion. But really, when you think about it, if God really is what we say He is, and we are what we are, how can we possibly have anything more than questions?"

Viktor lit a cigarette, ignoring Will's furrowed brow.

"It's always been good for me, church," Will continued. "Even when I wasn't sure why. Isobel never had any time for it, but still used to make me go. I think she recognised my need for it, saw the peace it brought me."

"So what happened?"

"I'm not sure. When she wasn't there to remind me that I needed it, I let it slip. And then…"

"And then."

The finality in how Viktor said those two words made Will's head swim. He suddenly experienced a sharp tang of saltwater in his mouth, and coughed, violently.

Viktor banged him on the back. "It's not time yet, champ. We've a while to tarry yet."

They sat there in silence for a minute or two. Will coughed again, trying to ignore the strong taste of salt.

"What was this for you then? Religion?"

Will considered. "I… I don't know."

"But you believed?"

"I never… didn't believe."

"Sounding pretty agnostic there," said Viktor, rubbing his youthful face, now lean again.

"I wasn't even certain of that. I don't think I was ever finely balanced enough to be agnostic, I always leaned heavily towards the side of belief. Not so much sitting on the fence, as standing very close to it, sometimes looking over. I mean, I had doubts, but…"

Viktor waited quietly for the thought to form and for Will to articulate it. The sun shone through the stained glass, giving the cool interior a beautiful sense of peace.

"I had doubts, but I think the one thing that held me was… You know when you arrive home, and you open the door and you call out, and when you don't get a response, sometimes you think you haven't been heard, but sometimes, there's something in the air that causes you to just know that the house is empty. Something in the echo. You know that? The difference between not getting a response, and there being no-one there to give you one?"

Viktor nodded.

"Well for me, that was my experience of prayer. I never once heard anything, never once received messages, or heard a voice. I never got a direct answer to a prayer in my life. And yet, I don't ever remember feeling like I was praying into the void. I never once felt stupid, like I was talking to myself. I never felt... not listened to. Never felt an absence."

"So your belief was based on the absence of an absence?"

Will smiled. "That's pretty much it. An absence of an absence. And once I'd accommodated myself to that, I just accepted that the Church was a man-made institution, but that what lay behind it, what it strived for, imperfectly, was something bigger than our comprehension that I didn't doubt. Ninety-five percent of the universe is unknown to us and unaccounted for, yet whatever that ninety five percent turns out to be, it's hypothesised that it binds the universe together in ways we can't begin to comprehend. So is the question really, Is there a God? Or should it only be, Is He sentient?"

Viktor looked at him quizzically. "Bit of a stretch."

"I'm not a theologian, a scientist. Or a philosopher."

"Then what are you?"

Will, who had been gazing out over the cloisters, drew his gaze back to Viktor, who was now fixing him with an unflinching, penetrating stare.

"Then," he repeated, "What. Are. You?"

12

Will's brain was whirling, he couldn't see anything, his mind was racing in circles. He had the sensation of being on his knees, and realised his hands were wet, as if he was on all fours in three inches of water. Was that sand beneath him? He vomited, the taste of saltwater now foul and overwhelming. He heard Viktor's question again and again, shouted now from somewhere behind him. "WHAT. ARE. YOU?" Will cried out that he didn't know, he begged it to stop, without any clear idea of what the question even meant. He was sick again, and his body started quivering, then shaking. His hands clenched tight, his weight bearing down through his arms onto his balled-up fists, he felt his fingernails bite into the soft flesh of his palms.

He was in a chair now, his chair, in his own front room in the house he'd shared...shared with Viktor.

No, not Viktor. Isobel. The house he'd shared with Isobel.

His fists were still tight, his body spasming, twitching, his shoulders jerking as if to throw his arms about with abandon, though they remained pressed hard against the arms of his chair. He tried to speak, to shout, but all he could force out from between his teeth were meaningless groans of anxiety...

An anxiety attack, he knew this. The smell of seawater disappeared and the small rational pilot sat in his head, which at times like this could still see the outside world, focussed on the familiarity. *You know what this is*, the pilot said. *You know this will pass. You know this is temporary. Any minute now, Isy will realise what's happening and be in here to comfort you and talk you down.* Except Isy isn't here. She's gone, and she doesn't do that anymore. *You're on your own now, and you don't have the tools to stop this, so this will get worse and worse until you pass out. You have put yourself in a position where this will knock you out, because you let Isy...*

Viktor snapped his fingers twice in Will's face, and the shock derailed the train of thought and suddenly Will was back in the room. Or not in the room. Back... on the hillside?

"It's okay, you're okay. You don't need to do that. I'm sorry. You're okay."

Will stared at Viktor. "I don't... know..."

As was often the way, Will had little to offer for quite some time other than those three words, repeated at intervals. Viktor watched him with, Will realised, concern. Funny, he thought, that part of his brain could be concerned about another part. Or was it? Maybe not. Will shook his head.

"A little anxiety episode there?"

"It... happens."

"Even now? That seems unfortunate."

Viktor was leaning against a roughly-carved rectangular block of stone, on which was fastened a plaque bearing a representation of the city's skyline, as seen from the hillside it was located on. A visual guide to help people identify the significant buildings in the panorama before them.

"It... Yes... I think... It seems unfair."

Viktor smirked. "Unfair? It's a weird idea, isn't it. The idea of life having any sense of fair play, any obligation to provide parity."

"There was a time I'd... That I'd argue that point."

"Really? You thought existence was subject to rules? To equal opportunity?"

"Equal opportunity doesn't have to mean equal outcomes. It just means equal opportunity. The same chance as someone to come good, not that you must both come good."

"Said with the casual indifference of privilege. But you wouldn't say that now?"

"I …" Will's shoulders slumped as he felt his mouth forming the same words, for the umpteenth time. He let the sentence hang there unfinished, unsaid. He didn't know.

The spring day was warm, there was a buzzing of insects nearby, amongst the flowering gorse. Will looked out over the city. There was no sign of movement from this distance, but then there never was. The absence of traffic noise was more striking.

"I think, the question of fairness doesn't get resolved one way or the other. I think it becomes irrelevant."

Viktor, drawing a cigarette from a crumpled packet, looked up at Will and scratched his greying beard. "Irrelevant?"

"Meaningless. Life isn't inherently fair or inherently unfair. It's just an absurd question."

"You're not wrong there."

"You remember that wrestling movie, the one with the family from round here?"

Viktor lit his cigarette and nodded. "Of course."

"They came up here a couple of times when a character wanted to realise something, thoughtfully. You know what I thought was amazing about that movie?"

71

"That anyone in Hollywood wanted to make a movie about this place?"

"Cheap. No, what I thought was extraordinary was that whilst on the surface it was a typical rags-to-riches, follow-your-dreams, achieve-your-destiny sports movie, it actually had the opposite message. Those movies always tell you that if you want something hard enough, and work at it hard enough, you can get it. All that stands between you and your dreams is your own desire and work ethic. But in this movie, you remember the main girl's brother? He wanted it just as much, if not more. Worked just as hard, if not more. Definitely was more committed. And he didn't get it. It just wasn't there for him. No matter how much he wanted it, and how hard he worked, the prize just wasn't on offer for him. Sometimes, you have no say in how well you do. Now, that's an honest sports movie."

"Bleak, though."

"That's reality. It *is* bleak."

"I'm not sure that's a given." Viktor eyed Will sideways, as he continued to look out over the city.

"But it is. There's no joy inherent in existence, only joy in what you can make from it. And the things it gives you to make joy from are not the same for everyone. If you're born in a Favela in Rio, you just don't have the opportunity to make anything of yourself. You could work your whole life and not even reach the starting point of a life like yours or mine. Mine," Will corrected himself.

The two men stood quietly for a moment. Then, from nowhere, a thought struck Will.

"You know the really depressing thing about Monopoly?"

A rather bemused expression on his face, Viktor gestured at him to explore this new direction. "Go on."

"You know within the first few goes, short of an incredibly unlikely late turnaround brought on by chance, who's going to win and who's going to lose. The game is effectively over. Yet there's a vast yawning chasm of time to fill between the game being over, and when it actually ends. It's about half an hour of competition, followed by two and a half hours of inevitable misery for everyone except the winner. That's Monopoly. And that's life. Short of a miracle, you know exactly how it ends long before it does. And nobody wants, in their recreation, to be reminded of how shitty their life is."

"So this is you," Viktor threw his hands up in a petulant gesture, "What? Tipping the board over, scattering all the pieces before the end, so you don't have to carry on to the finish, because you already know you've lost?"

Will looked straight at Viktor for the first time since they appeared on the hillside. "Maybe that's exactly what this is." His tone was almost defiant.

"That seems… childish."

Will shrugged. "And it's not like we ask to play."

Viktor turned to face Will in disbelief. "Did you just, in all seriousness, point out to me that you didn't ask to be born?"

"Say it how you like, it's true. I'm stuck in a game that I didn't choose to play, and can't hope to win. Isn't the logical choice to stop playing?"

"It depends how you define winning."

13

The floor felt damp under Will's feet, but just as he started to look down, he realised the implication of the sensation and, not wanting to face it, whipped his eyes up again. As he did so, the salty smell he'd noticed vanished.

He was in an auditorium, a theatre. In the circle, about halfway back. It was empty, aside from him and Viktor, who was sat on his row, with one seat between them. The auditorium didn't feel like an empty auditorium, however. There was a tangible air of attention, which Will assumed his mind was filling in, as if the stalls were full.

On the stage, a striking black woman, head shaved and impossibly lithe, was dancing, surrounded by half a dozen or so other dancers, who moved as if in worship of her. The woman was mesmerising, a breath-taking combination of grace and power. Will watched her, transfixed, suddenly oblivious to his surroundings. The routine unfolded, progressed, swelled and climaxed, and the auditorium was filled with the thunderous applause of the unseen audience below. Will, knowing this was nothing more than his imagination, or a memory, nevertheless clapped until his hands were sore.

"Remarkable, eh?" Viktor was lighting a cigarette as the houselights came up and there began a low rumble of activity.

"Stunning," agreed Will.

"You enjoy...?" Viktor waved the cigarette-holding hand at the stage, his gesture not so much indicating the performance in front of them, as the whole spectrum of performing arts.

"Very much." Will looked around at the auditorium, realising where they were. "I worked here for a while. Opened my eyes to a whole new world. Opera, drama, ballet, musicals... Dance like this though, I could watch for hours." He snapped his fingers as his memory provided him with the facts he had been seeking, and pointed at the now vacant stage. "Zeleidy Crespo, dancing Reinoso's *Satori*. I actually saw this one performed here. Crespo's an incredible dancer. I remember being blown away, she was just so captivating, I couldn't take my eyes off her." He took the cigarette Viktor offered him, and lit it. "I'd never seen anything like her."

"So how do you define winning?"

Will, at that moment inhaling from his cigarette, coughed and spluttered. "How do I... what?"

"Life's like Monopoly, you have to keep playing even when you know you're not going to win. How do you define winning?"

Will looked over at Viktor, who stared questioningly back from underneath his cap. His beard seemed fuller than ever, and the white was starting to outnumber the brown.

"Success?" Will hadn't ever thought about it in such concrete terms.

"Success? Worldly success? You measure winning financially?"

"No, of course not," replied Will, defensively. "I mean, I don't know, happiness? Satisfaction."

"But surely everyone is satisfied by different things."

"Well yes, that's... yes. What makes me happy isn't going to make you... I mean, well it will with you because..."

Viktor, cigarette in mouth, squinting from the smoke curling into his eyes, rolled his hand in a manner as if to say, Yes, yes, me, you, same thing, don't need to say it, carry on...

"But yes, everyone has their own definition of what a successful life is."

"So everyone can define their own happiness?"

"I suppose, if you…" Will sensed the trap, and attempted to sidestep it. "But ah, no. Defining happiness for yourself is not the same as achieving that definition."

"But surely, if you can define it for yourself, and you define it in such a way as to set a goal you can't reach, can you not redefine it? Set yourself a new goal."

"It isn't as simple as that."

"It isn't?"

"No. Can you choose what makes you happy? I don't think you can do that any more than you can choose to fall in love… anyway, why are we here, what has this to do with…" Will gestured at the stage.

"Seems to me you have a thing here that brings you great joy, and partaking of that enjoyment isn't an unattainable goal. You work, sure, and right now you're alone. But there's joy to be had, still, in the way you choose to live your life, the things you choose to experience."

"Redemption via the Arts?"

"If you like."

Will slumped in his seat and stared moodily down at the stage. "Maybe passive consumption of others' skills isn't enough."

"Maybe," countered Viktor. "But isn't it you who decides if it's enough or not?"

Will didn't answer.

The scene on stage grew hazy, and then suddenly focused again, and Will realised there was an orchestra on, tuning up. From the stalls, the hum of the audience indicated that they were settling in for the performance. The tuning finished, there was a pause and, after a moment, the brooding first movement of Tchaikovsky's *Manfred Symphony* began.

Viktor leaned over. "I love this one," he whispered.

Will nodded in agreement. It was a piece he had stumbled upon by chance, but it had stuck, and was one of his favourites, though he had never seen it performed live.

"Fitting, don't you think?" asked Viktor, again in a whisper.

"I don't know. Shh!"

Viktor leaned back in his chair, and flung an arm over the back of the seat between them. But he seemed restless, adjusting his position, crossing and recrossing his legs. Will sensed an eagerness on Viktor's part to talk and, though he longed for nothing more than to put all thought out of his mind and absorb the music, finally gave in. He nodded at Viktor and got up to leave.

In the bar outside, after a solitary anonymous figure poured them each a gin and tonic, Viktor led them out on to the balcony, and lit a cigarette.

It was dark outside, though the city was lit up as ever, and it was pleasantly warm. Will accepted a cigarette, and sipped his gin.

"So you don't think it's enough to just enjoy life, to have a satisfying, good life, doing the things you want. You need something else."

"When I was young," Will answered, "I thought my life would be defined by having a family of my own. I thought that was how you measured success, by the quality of the family you created and brought up."

"Sounds proscriptive. Surely not everyone can measure life that way?"

"I didn't see it as being universal, it's what success meant for me, where I thought I'd find a sense of achievement. Being a father."

"But you have no children."

"Obviously, you know that. And why. Look, why am I explaining this to you, you're supposed to be me. You are me."

"Yes, yes, yes, we've been over that. But clearly you want, even now, to get to the bottom of why you've done this. So. Fatherhood. The unattained dream."

Will relented. "No, not really. When I was young, I said. Later, I realised it wasn't something that I actually wanted. Or thought would be a good idea. One or the other."

"Not a good idea?"

"No."

"Because...?" Viktor let the word hang in the air, with an encouraging circular gesture of his hand.

"You know, reasons."

"Reasons?"

"Yes."

"Such as…?" Again, the hand invited expansion.

"Such as the environment, the population crisis, what having a child meant for the world, and what the world had to offer a child in the twenty-first century. Then there's my own weaknesses. Would I be a good father, would I pass on… this?" at which point Will tapped his temple forcibly, to indicate his own perceived mental and emotional weaknesses. "And Isobel. There were reasons."

"And therefore you couldn't achieve that success."

"Honestly, I'd stopped thinking of it in those terms by then. But I still wanted to make some mark. Some way that the world would … be better, for having me in it."

"Such as?"

"Such as," Will waved his hands uncertainly in front of him, but finally let them drop again. "I don't know."

"Ah."

"Yes."

Will inhaled and expelled a plume of smoke, dejectedly.

"So, you don't know what would have made your life worth living. But it wasn't enough to just live, to just *enjoy*. You wanted to *do*."

"I wanted to do."

"Hmm." Viktor leaned forward on the balcony, looking out onto the street, and the library beyond. After a moment, he took another sip of gin, and coughed. "Doesn't seem like a reason to kill yourself, mind."

"No," said Will. "No, it doesn't."

Viktor pulled abstractly at his jumper, and then scratched his beard. "I don't really know where to go from here."

"Do you want to talk about my schooldays?"

"Do you?"

"Good lord, no."

14

Will looked down at his hands and wondered why he was holding a book. He coughed, spluttered twice, and held the book out of the way as he suddenly expectorated a small quantity of seawater onto the carpeted floor beneath him. His trainers were sodden and his trousers were wet almost up to the knee.

Viktor, leant against a bookcase, one arm folded across his chest holding the elbow of the other, which in turn was raised and holding an inevitable cigarette, looked down at where Will had emptied his lungs. He raised his eyes up to look at Will again, and slowly brought a finger of his smoking hand to his lips. "Shhh. This is a library."

Will looked down at the book in his hands. The words 'Humankind cannot bear very much reality' jumped out at him, and he dropped it. Bracing himself against the book stack in front of him, he coughed up seawater again. "I can't... hardly..."

Viktor reached out and thumped him on the back a couple of times. Will's coughing finally eased, and he drew in a deep, uncertain breath.

"It's getting close, isn't it."

"It's getting close."

"I'm drowning."

"That was your aim, as I understood it."

"I hadn't expected to... be so aware of it."

"No, I don't imagine you had."

"Library?"

"Indeed."

"Importance of books?"

"Uh huh."

"Then...?"

"Thought it might cheer you up."

"No agenda?"

Viktor put out his arm again, and rested it in a manner suggesting of comfort on Will's back. "Now why would you imagine I have an agenda?"

"I presume I'm here so you can show me something. Isn't that your job as the Ghost of Suicides Present?"

"Hilarious."

"So. No life lessons to be learnt?"

Viktor removed his hand and eyed Will thoughtfully, and with a look that implied the thoughts were not of a pleasant nature.

"If you want this to be over…"

"That's the whole point."

"Fair enough."

15

For one horrible ghastly moment, there was nothing but blackness. A pressure in his ears, and Will realised his lungs were full of water. The taste of salt in his mouth, which he opened to scream, though no sound emerged. Frantically thrashing his limbs in the manner of a child's interpretation of what swimming might be, he suddenly found himself being jerked upwards. A hand was on his collar, which he in turn grabbed onto with both his hands, before suddenly his head broke clear of the water and something hard and uncomfortable jammed into his back. He swung there for a moment, the water just below his shoulders, coughing and holding on with all his might to the unseen arm. Then suddenly another hand grabbed him under his armpit, and with a sudden heave, and another uncomfortable jarring against his back, he was drawn up and over the gunwale of a small dinghy.

He fell into the bottom of the boat, and looked up at the man sat on the bench, his brown v neck jumper rolled up at the sleeves, and the brown flat cap pulled down tightly onto his head, a lit cigarette poking out from the bushy brown and white beard.

Will, wheezing and spluttering, pushed himself up onto his elbows. "You!"

Viktor removed the cigarette from his mouth, blew out a cloud of smoke, and grinned. "You were expecting someone else?"

Will suddenly realised it was daylight. "Then this is…"

"I'm afraid so. You're still going under."

"No, I … I wasn't looking to be… I just… where are we?"

Will looked around, and realised the boat was floating in the middle of a lake. There was no breeze, barely a ripple on the surface. The lake was small, about half a mile in length, and there was heavy vegetation on every bank, the occasional fishing platform projecting out into the water. Beyond the bushes in one direction lay a number of pyramid-like concrete structures.

"Ah, I see. I didn't think they allowed boating here."

"Probably don't. Seemed like a nice idea, though."

Viktor opened a bag that was slung on the floor

87

of the boat, and pulled out a packet of sandwiches, which he tossed at Will, who caught them one-handed, against his chest. Viktor was unwrapping his own sandwiches. He took one out, held it up to his nose, sniffed, and then frowned. "Hmm. I hope this ham isn't on the turn."

"Couldn't you…" Will waved his hand around in a circular motion, conveying the absurdity of his mind having conjured up a snack, and making that snack a bad sandwich.

Viktor looked up, his face suggesting that he had forgotten Will was there. "Eh? Oh. Hmm. I suppose." He looked decidedly glum. And tired. He suddenly looked very tired.

"Perhaps…"

"The running out of time and the decaying of the illusion?" Viktor sniffed the sandwich again and grimaced. "Very probably." He tossed the sandwich out of the boat, to the enthusiastic cheer of a nearby duck.

"So this is it?"

Viktor took one last look in the paper bag that contained the rest of his sandwiches, before throwing them all at the duck.

"Looks very much like it might be it."

"I have no particular attachment to this place, it seems odd that my mind would have chosen here to end it."

"What would you have chosen?"

Will pondered, only for a moment, before responding. "To do what I did this afternoon. This actual afternoon, I mean."

"Which was?"

"I re-watched *Playtime* for the final time."

"Ahh, Tati. Le grand homme."

"Indeed. His masterpiece."

"Undoubtedly. Bankrupted him, you know."

"Of course I know. How would you know if I didn't know?"

"Fair point."

"He once came 46th in a poll of the fifty greatest film directors of all time. But he only made six films! Six films! His exacting standards and the financial strain that went with them meant he didn't get the chance to make more."

"I would imagine that by some standards, he would hardly measure up as a successful director, then." Viktor's tone conveyed a certain slyness.

Will eyed Viktor shrewdly. "By some standards, I imagine he wouldn't. But returning to your question, that is how I'd choose to spend my time, before it ended." Will corrected himself. "It is how I spent that time."

"Re-watching *Playtime*."

"Re-watching *Playtime*."

"Retreating into the safe and familiar, instead of reaching out to the new and unusual."

"Yes."

"What happened to your ability to face change?"

"You know what happened."

"Pretend I don't."

"But you do! I do! We both know what happened!" Forgetting he was in a small boat, or perhaps just not caring, Will launched to his feet in exasperation, jabbing an accusing finger at Viktor. Viktor flinched back in surprise, and the boat rocked violently. Will's knees buckled, and he flung out his arms for something to grab, to steady himself. The only thing he could reach was Viktor. It didn't help as much as Will had hoped. The boat turned over.

16

The room was dark. Not pitch-black, just dark. A small, old television sat on an upturned packing crate, the screen a fuzz of interference. On a tired rug sat two tired old armchairs, and on the two tired old armchairs sat two tired men. One, his arms flopped over the sides of the chair and his legs stretched out in front of him, looked as if he were asleep with his cap down over his eyes, whilst in his mouth, protruding through a grey-white beard, was a cigarette, which periodically shifted slightly upwards and glowed as the man inhaled, before lowering again, a pair of smoky plumes exiting his nostrils. The other was huddled under a blanket, shivering slightly. His hair was wet.

It wasn't a large room, though if pushed, you would have to admit that the walls weren't entirely perceptible. The gloom was just enough that the edges of the visible part of the room were only a few feet away. The only light source was the snow-filled screen of the small television, so perhaps the rear wall would have been lit up, but sitting in the armchairs there was little else to see other than the rug, the television, the crate, and the small vase on top of the television with two or three dying flowers in it. The television was of an age that the top of it was large enough to usefully serve as a surface.

Two. Two dying flowers.

One of Viktor's arms reached up and took the cigarette from his mouth. The long, fragile extension of ash instantly fell off on to his brown jumper. The moving hand, still holding the cigarette, brushed ineffectually at the ash, spreading and rubbing it into the material, rather than removing it. Then it dropped the cigarette into a bottle that, suddenly, had been beside his chair all the time. The hand then moved back up and squirmed its way into his trouser pocket to draw out a crumpled pack of cigarettes. The other hand reached up and withdrew what turned out to be the last two cigarettes. One was inserted into Viktor's beard and eventually into his mouth. The other was tossed lightly onto Will's blanket. Viktor fumbled for a moment with the packet, before the realisation that it was empty led him to crumple it up and lob it, gracefully, over the television. Viktor lit his cigarette.

Will stared at his for a moment, before a hand snaked its way out of the intricacies of the blanket, took hold of it, reached up and put it in his mouth. The armchairs were close enough that with half a turn, Viktor could roll over and reach his arm to Will's mouth, lighting the cigarette for him.

For a couple of minutes, nothing happened.

"So what happened with Isobel?"

"Does it matter?" Will's voice was low, as though reluctant to be heard.

"I don't know. Does it?"

Will thought about this for a moment. "Do you know, I honestly don't think it does."

"Seems unlikely."

"Does it matter if I left? Or if she left? Or she died, or had a stroke, or realised she was a lesbian, or got a promotion and moved to Australia? Does it change the end of the story? Once, she was there. She was there, and all the chaos of the world was something I could live with. All those things, the myriad depressing absurd things about human behaviour, they were things we could despair of together, whilst we worked to make our own corner of life as pleasant a one as possible to live in. And then, one day, she wasn't there. The reasons and wherefores don't amount to a whole lot in the end, because it wasn't that she was gone, or why she was gone, it was because, with her being gone, the rest of it was just too much to bear. The scales, held in balance between the good and the bad, were no longer in balance, and the bad… tipped. Tea, chips, art, the beach, my home, nature, everything, even the fucking cigarettes were still in there. But the scales tipped, and I wasn't strong enough to even them up on my own. It's not enough to have things to live *for*, it's the things you have to live *with* that hold the power. And there was too much. There was just too, too much."

Viktor stood up slowly, stretched his arms and groaned softly under his breath. He scratched his beard, and then he scratched his arse. Taking a decisive step over to the television, he took one last, long drag on his cigarette and dropped it into the vase with the dying flowers. Then he turned to face Will, who looked up to return the gaze. There were tears on Will's face.

"It was just too much," he repeated, almost silently.

"Budge up."

The armchair that Will was curled up in was suddenly just that tiny bit bigger. Big enough for a slightly overweight man to drop in beside him, provided he angled himself slightly askew, and sat slightly raised. Viktor did just that, after taking the cigarette from Will's mouth and dropping it, causing it to hiss in the lapping seawater that now surrounded them. Gently, he put his arms around Will, pulling his head onto his chest.

"Another person is never the answer," Will's voice, hardly audible now, almost broke. "I know that. But that doesn't mean they can't make all the difference."

Viktor rested his chin lightly on the top of Will's head, stroking his arms as he held him.

"I just want it to be over."

"It won't be long now."

The television flickered, and a picture emerged from the fuzz. A tall, thin man, in a mac and hat, pipe in mouth, umbrella in hand, was in an airport.

He looked lost.

In the room, Will and Viktor lifted their feet out of the water and tucked them onto the chair.

"We've just a little time left."

THE END

James Kinsley lives in Norwich where he works for an arts-based charity. The desire to use his mental health issues creatively drives much of his writing, including his blog – unclekins.wordpress.com

He also publishes science fiction under the name Ray Adams.